Quest for El Dorado

by Lisa Thompson

sundance
A Haights Cross Communications Company

A Haights Cross Communications ® Company

Published by Sundance Publishing
One Beeman Road
P.O. Box 740
Northborough, MA 01532-0740
800-343-8204
www.sundancepub.com

First published as Treasure Trackers by
Blake Education, Locked Bag 2022, Glebe 2037, Australia
Exclusive United States Distribution: Sundance Publishing

Photography:
Cover Royalty-Free/Getty Images;
Back cover (compass) photos.com

ISBN-10: 1-4207-0721-3
ISBN-13: 978-1-4207-0721-2

Printed in China

contents

The Legend of El Dorado. 5

CHAPTER 1   Know Your Stuff 7

CHAPTER 2   On a Mission 12

CHAPTER 3   Jungle Trek 19

CHAPTER 4   The Surprise Visit. 27

CHAPTER 5   The Promise 32

CHAPTER 6   Their Only Chance 38

CHAPTER 7   Treasure to Protect. 43

Glossary 46

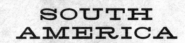

SOUTH AMERICA

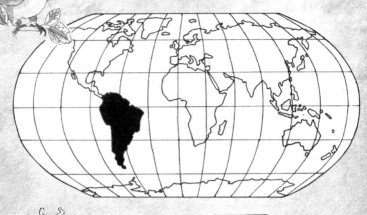

DR. SIMMONS CAMP

BRIDGE

WATERFALL

WHIRLPOOLS

CAPTIVE ISLAND

EL DORADO

EL DORADO

THE LEGEND OF EL DORADO

When the Spanish reached Colombia in the 16th century, they found the land inhabited by native people they named Indians. The Spanish first heard of the legend of El Dorado from the Indians of Columbia.

Legend said that somewhere in the jungle was a kingdom rich in gold and precious stones. When a new ruler was appointed, he would cover himself in powdered gold and appear before his people by a lake. He would float on a raft to the center of the lake. Then he would throw gold and precious stones into the water as offerings to their god.

Today it is believed that the legend was based on a ceremony performed by the people who lived around Lake Guatavita.

Many tried to find the riches of El Dorado, but the kingdom was never found. Although El Dorado remained undiscovered, large quantities of gold and jewels were plundered and taken from other native peoples. Entire tribes and cultures were wiped out.

MAP OF THE AMAZON

Venezuela

Guyana
Suriname
French
Guiana

Colombia

Atlantic Ocean

Ecuador

Peru

Brazil

Bolivia

Pacific Ocean

Paraguay

Argentina   Uruguay

Chile

N
W   E
S

CHAPTER 1

Know Your STUFF

Uncle Earl raced across the top of the canyon
to meet Ramón and Mia. "Up here!" he called. "You
made it! I just knew you could do it! It was a piece
of cake, right?"

Mia reached the top of the canyon, hauled

herself over using her last bit of energy, and fell to the ground, exhausted. She was covered in dirt and scratches. Her teeth were clenched. Mia was more than angry. She was about to EXPLODE!

"Uncle Earl! Are you kidding me! I can't believe you made us do that! It was the most difficult . . ."

"Stop! Wait, Mia!" Ramón shouted, as he climbed the last few rocks. Ramón knew his best friend was about to say something she would regret. The four-hour hike, followed by the three-hour climb, had taken its toll.

Uncle Earl had told them that they would be jumping out of a plane. He'd told them about the parachutes. But he hadn't mentioned the long hike and the climb! Only after they reached the ground did they find a note from Uncle Earl, along with a small map.

"Uncle Earl," said Ramón breathlessly, "that hike was a killer!"

Mia cut in sharply. "Uncle Earl! What were you

thinking? That was no ordinary hike. The jungle was so thick we could have been lost forever!"

"Oh, come on. I knew you two could do it," he beamed. "I never doubted you for a moment!"

Ramón was still trying to catch his breath. The difficult hike had been a test. He knew how Mia's uncle's mind worked. Uncle Earl wanted them to get a taste of what the Amazon jungle was like. Uncle Earl wasn't the expert's expert in archaeology by chance. Ramón had heard his motto many times. *It's all in the details!*

Mia wasn't giving in that easily. "Dropping us in the middle of NOWHERE and making us hike out? Have you gone NUTS? Look at me, I'm scratched from head to toe! Anyway, I know all about jungle survival. I didn't need to go through that again. I've read *101 Tips If You Get Lost in the Amazon* THREE times!"

Ramón laughed. Mia could be such a drama queen. "I told you to follow me," he said. "But no— you had to go your own way. That spiky bush you walked into had your name written all over it."

"Now, Mia," said Uncle Earl calmly, with just a hint of a chuckle, "if you are coming with me on this expedition, you must learn how to look after yourself. You must be prepared—even though nothing can *really* prepare you for the Amazon. It's another world. It's no ordinary jungle. Everything about it is so big."

"Like spiders as big as my head," teased Ramón.

"With bigger brains!" Mia snapped back.

Uncle Earl continued, "When you are going as far into the jungle as we are, you need to know all about survival. And not just from books, Mia. If you get lost, I need to know that you have the will to survive—just in case."

"In case of what?" asked Ramón.

Mia cut in. "In case you get bitten on the knee by a scorpion, or wrapped up tight by a huge boa constrictor, or giant termites bite you all over, and you have to beg me to save you!"

Ramón laughed. "Mia, you crack me up when you're angry."

Uncle Earl glanced at his watch. "I must say you two got here in very good time."

"That's because I had a little help." Mia grinned and pulled out her gadgets—a compass and a high-tech, state-of-the-art global positioning system.

"Hard to get lost with those," said Uncle Earl.

Mia nodded. "Always expect the unexpected."

Uncle Earl laughed proudly.He had taught Mia well.

Ramón felt his energy creeping back. "So when do we head for the Amazon?"

"Why, this very moment!" Uncle Earl pointed to a helicopter flying over the canyon toward them. "Here's our ride. Dr. Simmons and his team are waiting for us. We should be there by nightfall."

•

CHAPTER 2

ON a Mission

The view from the air was amazing. Tall trees made a canopy blocking any view of the ground. Occasionally an even taller tree reached up higher toward the sun. From the chopper, the forest looked like a carpet of trees with rivers winding through it like long snakes. They found a clearing and landed the helicopter. The rest of the journey had to be made by boat.

As they went deeper and deeper into the rain forest, Uncle Earl, Ramón, and Mia left their world behind. Strange sounds, plants, and smells surrounded them. Ramón and Mia had an eerie feeling that a thousand pairs of eyes were watching them as they motored upriver.

After rounding another bend in the river, Dr. Simmons's camp came into view on the riverbank. It was basic—just a few tents, some hammocks with mosquito nets, a table sheltered by a roof of leaves, and some giant fallen logs for chairs.

They pulled the boat onto the shore and saw Dr. Simmons sitting at a table studying some stone carvings. Dr. Simmons believed that the carvings belonged to a tribe of Indians who had lived here long ago. But that was not the reason that Dr. Simmons had called Uncle Earl. He needed Uncle Earl's help with a much more important matter.

Dr. Simmons was a fidgety man with a lined and weathered face. He had spent most of his life outdoors. He talked rapidly as they entered the camp.

"Thanks for coming, Earl, and thanks to you, too, Ramón and Mia. What do you think of the jungle so far? It's amazing, isn't it?"

"Your message sounded truly fascinating, Dr. Simmons," said Uncle Earl. "A sighting of the Golden Man from El Dorado? If it's true, and you can find him—wow! It would be one of the richest and rarest finds ever!"

Dr. Simmons nodded in excited agreement, his eyes wide. Sweat trickled down his face. In fact, sweat trickled off all of them. And for the first time, Ramón and Mia noticed how hot and heavy the air was. A few seconds later, it started to rain. Big, heavy raindrops pelted down and started bouncing off them.

"Let's take cover," Dr. Simmons said as he moved them toward the sheltered table. "You'll get used to being wet soon enough." He cleared the table and spread out a large map. "Come, sit down and look at the map. Let me explain."

Mia studied the map closely before whispering to Ramón, "There's the camp marked on the map. Look how many rivers crisscross this area."

"Yeah! And by the looks of things, we're a long, long way from civilization," Ramón replied.

Dr. Simmons began his story. "About a month ago, I was walking alone in the jungle. I came upon an Indian man from a tribe I had never seen before. He looked unusually tall and strong. A large, golden breastplate was hanging from chains around his neck. It was exquisite! As I glanced at it, I realized that it was engraved with the symbol of El Dorado."

Dr. Simmons handed the golden breastplate to Uncle Earl.

"How on earth did you get it?" Uncle Earl asked.

"When I showed interest in it, the man gave it to me. Then he ran off," Dr. Simmons answered. "When I returned to camp with it, some of my team believed it was a sign of bad luck, and they fled. Many had heard terrible stories about the fierce warriors of El Dorado. I had to get a whole new team out here. Luckily, I met Sipu. He agreed to be my headman, and he found some men to help me."

"Who is Sipu?" asked Uncle Earl curiously.

Dr. Simmons pointed to a strong and proud Indian who wore gold crescents through his ears. The man was busy talking to his team, but he had one eye on the new members of the camp.

"Have you seen the man from El Dorado again?" asked Mia.

"Yes. I saw him about a week ago, by a river not far from here. I was alone again." Dr. Simmons dropped his voice and began to whisper. "I saw him washing gold dust off himself! When he saw me, he ran off—but he left this behind." Dr. Simmons handed Uncle Earl a small, golden figure of a man. Mia and Ramón were completely spellbound.

"So, what do you think about it, Earl?" asked Dr. Simmons.

"Well . . . it has similar markings to other gold figures believed to be from El Dorado." Uncle Earl smiled and said, "Dr. Simmons, I have a very good feeling about this!"

"What exactly is El Dorado?" asked Ramón, barely able to take his eyes off the gold.

Dr. Simmons still spoke in a whisper. "It is believed to be an ancient kingdom where everything was made of gold."

Uncle Earl broke in. "Legend has it that once a year the king covered himself in gold dust and became the Golden One. *El Dorado* means *Golden One.* The king sat upon a raft laden with gold and precious stones and was rowed to the middle of a great lake. The Golden One then threw his riches into the lake as an offering to the gods."

"Is that who you think you saw in the forest?" asked Mia.

"Yes." Dr. Simmons's eyes were gleaming.

"Awesome! Sounds like my kind of kingdom!" said Ramón.

"Hang on." Mia had found a hitch. "Has anyone ever been to El Dorado and returned? Or is it some sort of secret, lost city?"

"Young lady," Dr. Simmons replied curtly, "the jungle holds many secrets that it does not give away easily." He waved his fingers across the map of the jungle and pointed to a dark green, uncharted area. "I believe El Dorado and all its riches lie in this area. But enough excitement. You must rest now. Tomorrow we will begin our search for the golden kingdom of El Dorado."

CHAPTER 3

Jungle
TREK

They left the camp the next morning, just after first light. The forest canopy blocked out most of the sunlight. There was a thick fog on the ground that Sipu called a "cloud forest." They couldn't even see their feet as they walked.

Dr. Simmons led the way, slashing a path through the leaves and vines with his machete. The others followed behind. It didn't take long for the giant, hungry mosquitoes to come out and start biting them. Ramón couldn't stand it.

"They're chewing me up! There's going to be no blood left in me if they don't stop," he cried.

"Here, rub some of this on yourself." Mia handed him some insect repellent. She had stashed it in her survival belt, along with a compass, a fishing line, two flares, some waterproof matches, a pencil, and some chocolate.

"Thanks, Mia. I should've known you'd have something to help."

Suddenly, Sipu sank down to the ground and signaled for them to do the same. He had heard a noise up ahead. They all hugged the ground, not making a sound. Ramón's mind raced. Was it a jaguar, a monkey, that giant boa constrictor Mia had told him about—or was it the Golden Man?

His thoughts were broken by the crack of a twig. It was coming closer, whatever it was. Ramón held his breath and watched Sipu.

Sipu was as still as a rock, his head forward like a lizard's so he could hear every sound. An army of giant-sized ants moved up and down Sipu's arm, biting him. They were making lunch out of him, but Sipu didn't flinch. Finally, Sipu gave the all-clear signal and waved them on.

"What was that all about?" asked Mia.

Sipu pointed to the ground. There was a large paw print.

"Jaguar?" asked Uncle Earl, taking a look.

Sipu nodded. "We were lucky. He didn't smell us because we were downwind."

"Lucky for him or for us?" said Dr. Simmons unpleasantly. "Now let's get moving. This isn't a walk in the park, Sipu. Come on! Let's not waste more time." He marched off, setting a fast pace. "Hurry up, the rest of you!"

"I don't know what his hurry is. He's in a terrible mood," said Uncle Earl. "I'll go ahead and try to calm him down. You two walk behind us with Sipu."

"I think you should walk with us," Sipu suggested to Uncle Earl. "It will be safer. I will take good care of you."

"Don't you worry about me, Sipu. I'll be all right. I'll see you when you catch up!" Uncle Earl said. They watched as he disappeared ahead of them into the jungle.

"Sipu," said Mia, "your arm must be killing you. Those giant ants were eating you alive!"

Sipu just smiled. He broke off a branch and squeezed the sap onto the bites. Then he crushed some red berries from another plant and smeared the red pulp on his arm.

"You should wipe some of this on your skin, too," he said, giving them some berries. "It will keep most bugs away. It works much better than that cream you have."

Mia rubbed the berries evenly over her skin. Ramón painted himself with red stripes down his arms and legs and across his face.

"How do I look, Sipu?" asked Ramón. "Like a jungle boy?"

Sipu nodded and laughed. "Sure—but now come follow me. I will show you how to survive in the jungle. We will go this way."

Sipu made walking through the jungle look easy. This was his home. He had grown up here. He thought nothing of climbing over tree roots double his height, breaking vines for a quick drink, and climbing up a tree for a bite to eat. He walked so lightly through the forest that his feet barely left any marks on the ground. He showed Mia and Ramón how to walk through the rain forest without being seen or heard.

Sipu showed them how to recognize tracks of different animals. He showed them things to look for, such as a flick of dust left by a snake or a mark on a tree left by a monkey. He also told them important things to listen for, like the sounds of different birds and the noises made by various kinds of insects.

Sipu could tell just from the rustle of leaves which animal was passing by. He pointed out that the sounds made by a monkey in a tree were different from those made by a jaguar hunting for food.

Sipu showed them the plants to avoid. Some plants were as sharp as razor blades. Others were soft and smooth, yet very, very strong. He showed them which vines and leaves to use as rope. And as they kept on walking, they began to feel more at home in the rain forest.

"Oh, look at this. How cute!" Mia bent down to pick up a tiny green and black frog.

"No!" yelled Sipu. "Do not touch it!"

Mia froze.

"Sipu," said Ramón, "relax. It's just a little green frog. How dangerous could it be?"

Sipu moved them away. "That is a poison arrow frog. It's very dangerous. We use the poison from this frog on our arrow tips. It is deadly."

"That little frog?" asked Mia in disbelief.

"Come," said Sipu. "It's not far now. Just over this bridge."

"What bridge?" asked Mia. "I don't see any bridge here."

"You mean that bunch of vines?" cried Ramón. "Cool! It looks just like a tightrope."

The bridge of vines stretched over a deep ravine in front of them. The roar of water echoed all around them.

"Man, that has to be at least a hundred-foot drop!" Ramón shouted, taking a look over the edge.

"There's no way I'm walking across those vines, Sipu!" cried Mia. "Can't we go another way?"

"There is no other way," said Sipu, pointing to the bridge. "This is the only way."

"It'll be OK, Mia. I'll be right behind you, and

Sipu will be in front," said Ramón.

Mia stepped onto the bridge. She didn't look down. "No pranks, OK, Ramón? This isn't the time to horse around!"

Ramón took one of her hands, and Sipu reached out and took the other. They walked along the bridge, step-by-step. Suddenly the vines beneath them swung wildly. They lost their footing and fell down into the deep water below.

"AHHHHHHHHHHH!" cried Mia and Ramón.

Sipu just smiled as he plunged after them into the gushing river.

CHAPTER 4

The Surprise VISIT

The water carried them at a rapid pace over the edge of a roaring waterfall. Mia and Ramón tumbled and turned with the white water, gasping for air when they could, until the river carried them onto its bank.

"Awesome!" cried Ramón, shaking water out of his ears. "That waterfall drop blew away every roller coaster I've ever ridden. Hey, Mia?"

Mia was on her feet, looking at the riverbank. "What's this?" She dug a golden figure out of the mud. "Look, Ramón, it's another of those golden figures." This time the figure was standing on a raft.

"Did you enjoy your little ride?" asked Sipu from the bank above them.

"Oh! That was unreal. That bit just before we went over the edge . . ." Suddenly Ramón noticed what Sipu was wearing. "Hey, where did you get that crazy gold headdress, Sipu?"

"Your body is covered in gold," gasped Mia.

"Welcome to El Dorado." Sipu smiled. "I'm sorry about the bridge, but there is no other way to get here."

"YOU'RE the Golden Man who Uncle Earl and Dr. Simmons are looking for!" gasped Mia.

Sipu laughed and nodded. "Come, let me show you around. I must cover your eyes while I lead you into the village." He wrapped a blindfold made of spun gold around each of their heads.

They could still recognize the chirps and whistles of the forest animals and birds, but they couldn't see a thing. Ramón heard a rustle of leaves following them. "What's that?"

"Just the monkeys that live around the village. They are rushing to tell the villagers we have visitors. You will meet them soon."

After Sipu allowed them to remove their blindfolds, Ramón and Mia saw that El Dorado was even more amazing than Dr. Simmons's description. Everything around them was made of gold and glittered brightly in the sunlight.

Gold statues surrounded the doorways. Golden pots and water jugs hung inside homes. Baskets woven with gold fibers sat on the ground. Men, women, and children wore necklaces and earrings made of gold. And all over the ground, nuggets of gold and precious gems lay like pebbles.

"I can't believe how much gold is here!" cried Ramón. "You guys are loaded!"

"Here in El Dorado, we do not see gold in the same way as you do, Ramón."

"What do you mean, Sipu?" asked Mia.

"We have so much gold, we don't see it as something of great value. But we do see it as a thing of great beauty. Be careful, Mia. Leaning on our sun god could bring bad luck."

"Oh, sorry," said Mia, standing up straight.

"You see, the riverbeds and mountains that surround us are full of gold. As long as there is gold, the great sun god will protect our home—the rain forest. We bring gold to the sun god, and this pleases him. As long as we keep the sun god happy, my people and the rain forest will be protected."

"So, what's more valuable than gold in El Dorado?" asked Ramón.

Sipu smiled, and his eyes widened. "Let me show you the great treasures of El Dorado!" He clapped his hands. Immediately, three servants dressed in golden cloth brought golden plates laden with food and golden jugs spilling over with juice.

They dined on all sorts of rain forest delicacies, including fruit salad with peach palm, papaya, and honey. There were fish of every size, flowers you could eat, and nuts the size of apples. They drank all kinds of exotic juices. Everything was fresh and ripe, and each mouthful was delicious.

"I can't believe you get all this from the rain forest," said Mia.

"I can't wait until Uncle Earl gets here. He's going to love this place," said Ramón.

Mia had totally forgotten about Dr. Simmons and Uncle Earl.

Sipu's happy face turned grim. "Your uncle and Dr. Simmons must never find this place!"

Mia and Ramón looked at each other. What did he mean by that?

CHAPTER 5

The Promise

After they ate, Sipu showed them through the village. It was alive with activity. Women were cooking and playing with their children. Men were busy melting and hammering gold. There were cautious but friendly looks from the natives.

Ramón and Mia could not understand the language, but there was lots of laughter and chatter. Some children who were returning from the forest giggled and pointed at Ramón and Mia.

"What's so funny?" asked Ramón.

"The children are laughing at your berry stripes," Sipu said. "They think you have been bitten all over."

Ramón went a shade of pink and looked down at his stripes. Even the rushing water of the river hadn't washed off the pulp from the red berries.

As they walked through the village, Ramón couldn't keep his eyes off the bows and arrows the villagers carried. They were almost as big as the men themselves.

"Would you like to try one, Ramón?" asked Sipu, noticing his longing look.

"Awesome! I'd love to."

Ramón picked up a bow and arrow. Struggling, he said, "This is much heavier than it looks!" He tried to pull back on the bow, but it didn't move. "Are you sure this thing isn't locked?" he asked, pulling again without success.

"Give it up, Muscles," teased Mia.

Sipu took the bow, lifted it into the air, and shot an arrow with ease, high and far into the forest.

"It takes practice," said Sipu. "The strength of a great hunter is more than muscle."

They sat in the center of the village in an open dwelling. It was obvious Sipu had something important to tell them. "For hundreds of centuries, men from outside the forest have tried to find El Dorado. They do not care for the forest, for my people, or for the way we live. They do not care for our culture. They only want to steal our gold. Dr. Simmons is one such man. He has been in this area for many years looking for El Dorado and its gold."

"But I thought he was studying stone carvings," said Ramón.

"Dr. Simmons is a man whose word cannot be trusted. He does not understand the ways of the forest. He does not care for the people of El Dorado. You have to understand the power of gold. Dr. Simmons cares only for the wealth the gold will bring him back in your world.

The gold breastplate that he showed you was not given to him. He stole it from one of my people. Dr. Simmons is a greedy man. If he finds the gold, he will take it all. Then the sun god will no longer protect us, and the rain forest and our home will be destroyed. We cannot let him find us."

"But, Sipu, you work for Dr. Simmons. What were you doing in the camp in the first place?" asked Mia.

"I joined Dr. Simmons to make sure he would never find us. Then you and your uncle arrived. That night the sun god sent me a dream and told me it was you two who could help save my people."

Ramón was confused. "What can we do?"

"You can try to convince Mia's uncle to lead Dr. Simmons away from this area," said Sipu.

"Where is my uncle now?" asked Mia quietly.

"He and Dr. Simmons are being held captive on an island," answered Sipu.

"Captive!" cried Ramón. "They're prisoners?"

"They have been captured by our warrior guards who protect the kingdom. Everyone who tries to enter El Dorado faces the same fate. I tried to warn your uncle, but . . ."

Mia shivered. "Fate? What do you mean, Sipu?"

"When the sun sets tonight, the guards will look for a sign. If the sky turns golden, they will die. If the sky does not turn golden, Dr. Simmons and your uncle will be set free." His voice was matter-of-fact.

"Sipu!" cried Mia. "The sky here is golden at EVERY sunset."

"He's Mia's uncle! You have to help, Sipu,"

demanded Ramón.

"I will help you save what you love, if you will help me save what I love. I cannot stop this myself, but I will show you how you can. What happens to Mia's uncle and Dr. Simmons is then up to you. But you must promise me one thing."

"Anything, Sipu!" cried Ramón. "Anything!"

"I want your word that when you get back home, you must do everything you can to protect our rain forest. NEVER tell anyone what you have seen here. If you do, our world will surely be destroyed."

"You have our word," said Ramón, shaking Sipu's hand. "We promise to do everything we can."

Mia nodded in agreement. "Yes, and we will never breathe a word to anyone that we have been here. Please, Sipu, take us to Uncle Earl. The sun is getting low, so we don't have much time left."

CHAPTER 6

Their ONLY Chance

The three looked at the island and ten fierce-looking warriors. Dr. Simmons and Uncle Earl were bound to two trees by thick vine ropes.

Mia murmured softly, "How are we going to get them out of this?"

Sipu lowered his voice to a whisper. "Listen carefully, my friends. In a short time, the sky will turn the color of gold. All the warriors will drop to the ground to give thanks to the sun god. This is called the Golden Time, and it is your only chance to free Uncle Earl and Dr. Simmons. You must be as silent and as quick as possible, for it only lasts a few minutes. You must be like a jaguar eyeing his prey. Use these two pieces of sharp stone to cut the vines. There's a raft under those bushes. Jump on it, and leave immediately!"

"But will we be safe on the raft? Won't the warriors come after us?" Mia asked nervously.

"In this part of the river at Golden Time, the tide rises very quickly, creating great rapids and whirlpools around the island. If you reach the raft as the tide is rising and push it into the rapids, you have a good chance of making it downstream to safety. The warriors will not enter the water because of the whirlpools. But you must get to the raft as quickly as you can. If you take too long, the whirlpools will trap you on the banks of the island. Good luck, my friends. I will be watching. Remember—not only does the fate of Uncle Earl and Dr. Simmons rest in your hands, but also that of my people."

Sipu handed them two straw-like reeds. "Use these to get air when you are swimming underwater to the island. Hug the bottom like a slippery eel, and remember everything that I have shown you. Listen carefully, and keep your eyes open. Go quickly now! Here comes the Golden Time."

Ramón and Mia slid into the water without making a ripple. When they stepped onto the island, the warriors were all kneeling to the sun god. Uncle Earl spotted Mia and Ramón instantly. Ramón moved silently as Sipu had shown him, cut the rope, and swiftly led Uncle Earl to the raft. Mia freed Dr.

Simmons, showed him the raft, and led the way.

The Golden Time was almost over. Mia reached the raft. The tide was rising. Whirlpools and rapids started to appear.

"Where is Dr. Simmons?" asked Ramón.

"He was with me a minute ago," said Mia.

Mia turned and gasped. "Oh, no!" Dr. Simmons was kneeling on the ground, stashing gold nuggets into a bag and into his pockets as fast as he could. He collected the last of the gold nuggets and heaved the bag onto his shoulder. The warriors saw him and angrily gave chase.

"They're going to get him!" yelled Mia. The raft swirled around in the water with the force of the whirlpool. The warriors heard Mia's voice and turned toward them.

"Cut the vine, Mia! Cut the vine!" cried Ramón.

Mia cut the vine and set the raft free. "But what about Dr. Simmons?" yelled Mia, as arrows and spears flew toward them.

"He made his choice," yelled Uncle Earl. "Now, lay low and hang on tight!"

They clung desperately to the raft as it tossed and turned in the rapids.

"I think I hear a waterfall," shouted Ramón.

The water roared, and they shot over the edge. After being tossed about by the current, they landed on the bank of the river. Uncle Earl lay motionless on the muddy riverbank.

"Uncle Earl! Are you all right?" Mia cried.

Ramón looked over Mia's shoulder waiting for Uncle Earl to stir. Slowly, Uncle Earl opened his eyes and let out a little laugh.

"Oh, my. Wasn't that a ride and a half?" Uncle Earl said as he struggled to get up.

"Don't move, Uncle Earl," instructed Mia. "You have a cut on your head that I'm going to fix." She applied some mud from the riverbank to the cut. "There, that should be OK for now."

CHAPTER 7

Treasure to Protect

Uncle Earl felt his forehead. "You are quite a jungle girl after all, Mia. And Ramón . . ." He laughed a little harder. "Next time we shoot over a waterfall, try to act a little scared. You loved it so much, anyone would have thought you'd done it before!"

Ramón looked at Mia for help. "Only at an amusement park, Uncle Earl," she said.

But Uncle Earl wanted answers to bigger questions. "How did you two find us? Where did Sipu go? How did you know about that raft?"

Mia did what she did best and quickly changed the subject. "What about Dr. Simmons?" she asked.

"Hmm." Uncle Earl shakily got to his feet. "Dr. Simmons was . . . well, let's say he wasn't exactly after what he said he was after. Greed is a terrible thing. It can make great treasures worthless and destroy wonderful discoveries."

"I guess some treasures aren't meant to be found," said Mia.

"How true that is, Mia," sighed Uncle Earl.

Ramón noticed that the river had become calm. "We had better get going. We have a long way to go."

They set the raft afloat again and started down the river, listening to the whistles, chirpings, and clickings of the rain forest. The sounds reminded

Mia and Ramón just how wonderful and mysterious the rain forest truly was.

"Hey, look, guys!" cried Ramón, pointing to the sky. It was dark now, and the moon sat full in the night sky. It looked strangely golden. "Doesn't that look awesome?"

"Look at our skin," said Mia, lifting her arm.

The strange-colored moonlight was making them all look golden. El Dorado was with them. Ramón and Mia thought about Sipu and his secret tribe and the great gift that he had given them. He had shown them some of the real treasures of the rain forest. They would keep their word and do whatever they could to protect it. Their visit to El Dorado would remain a treasured secret forever.

THE END

glossary

breastplate armor worn to protect the chest

canopy the leafy branches of rain forest trees forming a dense cover

canyon a narrow river valley with steep sides

crescents curved shapes that taper to two points

El Dorado a legendary city of South America containing great treasure

exotic strikingly unusual, strange

exquisite of rare beauty, superbly made

fate destiny; fortune

flares devices that produce a brightly colored flame; used as a signal in an emergency

global positioning system a device that can work out exact coordinates of where you are in the world. It works by bouncing your signal off a satellite.

hammocks pieces of net or canvas hung between two supports

machete a large, heavy knife with a wide blade

motto a phrase or sentence that is a rule for a
person's behavior

nugget a small lump of gold

ravine a long, narrow valley shaped by water

ripple little waves on the surface of calm water

spellbound fascinated, entranced

survival able to go on living in spite of great
danger or difficulties

tribe a group of people of the same race, who have
the same language, beliefs, and customs

whirlpools small areas in a river or sea where
the water swirls quickly around and around.
Objects floating nearby are pulled into the
center.

more titles

Hunting Down the Grail

Quest for El Dorado

Missing Among the Pyramids

Search for the Lost Cavern

The Wreck of the Atocha

The Red Rain of Easter Island

Key of the Mayan Kingdom

Protecting the Sunken City